Sporting Relations

by the same author

Frinck, and Summer with Monika (Michael Joseph)
Watchwords (Cape)
After the Merrymaking (Cape)
Out of Sequence (Turret Books)
Gig (Cape)

Roger McGough

SPORTING RELATIONS

with drawings by
Terry Gilliam

 Eyre Methuen

First published in 1974 by Eyre Methuen Ltd
11 New Fetter Lane London EC4P 4EE
Copyright © 1974 by Roger McGough
Illustrations © 1974 by Terry Gilliam
Reprinted 1980

Printed in Great Britain by
Whitstable Litho Ltd, Whitstable, Kent

ISBN 0413 32750 7 (Hardback)
    0413 32760 4 (Paperback)

Whenever I feel in need of exercise, I put on a track suit and write poems about athletics. For the opportunity of being able to do this as Poetry Fellow at the University of Loughborough, I wish to thank Dr A.M. Duncan, the staff and students there.

Contents

Grandmama
(who was the All England
Cartwheeling Champion
1934—39) met
grandpapa
at a Rotary Club Luncheon.

He was a somersaulter.

Uncle Fergie
was a famed caber tosser.

As a caber tosser
he had no peer.

It is rumoured
he could toss a caber

to here.

from there

Cousin Caroline
was a very fine
sprinter. In the winter
of 1968, with a
bandaged knee
she ran the 100
metres in 10.3.

But her best time
was in the dressing room afterwards.

Jennifer Chubb-Challoner
the Cheltenham Ladies
Triple Jump Champion

was first spotted
by a peepingtom talentscout
while still at Junior School

when she won
the 3-legged race
all on her own.

Albert Robinson
(a half-cousin by marriage)
is probably the only
bullfighter in Birmingham.

At five in the afternoon
he parades round the Bull Ring
in his Suit of Lights
(an army battledress
and panty tights
sequinned plimsolls
and padded flies)
a faraway look
in his faraway eyes.

For he struts beneath
Andalusian skies
as concrete corridors
echo the cries
of aficionados
in shoppers' disguise
'El Robbo, El Robbo el mas valiente matador!'

On his way to the hostel
he stops and he buys
a carton of milk
and two meat pies
then it's olé to bed
and olé to rise.

Uncle Anthony
was a low hurdler.
Being only 4′ 6″
he was the lowest
hurdler in Bridlington.

In his summer of '42
he married a Northern Counties
high jumper, who, delighted to please,
being 2 foot taller,
straddled him with ease.

Uncle Malcolm
put the shot
for Scotland.

When he retired
he collected shots
as a hobby.

At the time
of his death
he had nearly 200.

And in accordance
with his last wishes
they were buried with him

at St Giles cemetery in Perth.
Uncle Mal is now at rest
somewhere near the centre of the earth.

Cousin Chas,
an expert in the art
of self-defence,
would go out of his way
to defend himself.

'In dis age of
senseless violence'
he would explain,
'one must be
equipped to meet
de aggressor
on his own grounds.'
He drank barley wine and guinness
and never bought rounds.

Every Saturdaynight
after a few pints
Chas and his mates
would roam the streets
looking for pale young men
against whom
they would defend themselves.

Cousin Chas
may not have been
one of Nature's gentlemen
but he was a right bastard.

Aunty Dora
was some highdiver.

People came
from miles around
to see her jackknives.

In 1965
although 8 months pregnant
she won the Bootle and District
High Diving Championship
for the third successive year.

No mean achievement.

Uncle Jed
Durham bred
raced pigeons
for money.

He died
a poor man
however

as the pigeons
were invariably
too quick for him.

Kung Fu Lee
a greenbelt
with a reputation second to none
was more than vexed
when annexed
and one morning built upon.

Uncle Bram
a batcatcher of distinction
scorned the use of
battraps, batnets and batpoison.
'Newfangled nonsense'
he would scoff, and off
he would go
to hang upsidedown
in belfries
for days on end
in the hope of snatching
one of the little batstards.

Billy our Kid
was the dandy
of the billiard rooms.
He affected
brocade waistcoats
of uncertain hue
and with his trusty
pearlhandled cue
hustled many an
amateur passerthrough.

In '59 he went to New Orleans
to try his luck.
Now he lives in Pittsburgh
and drives a truck.

Uncle Milo
a grandpiano of a man
threw hammers for Lincolnshire.

He trained on the Wolds
and seldom caught colds.

On his back
he had tattooed
a recipe for
stoat and mushroom pie.
Nobody knew why.

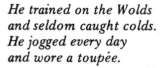

He trained on the Wolds
and seldom caught colds.
He jogged every day
and wore a toupée.

When not throwing
his weight about
he was a tug o'
warmonger.
With him it was
tugtugtug
all the time.
Uncle Milo
was a bugger ofa tugger.

He trained on the Wolds
and seldom caught colds.
He jogged every day
and wore a toupée.
He won many cups
and he died in them.

Uncle Mo
a shy bachelor of 43
was a nudist at heart.

Suddenly last summer
he formed a club
for bashful sunworshippers

who met in his
greenhouse every weekend
dressed to the nines.

Quiet as tomatoes
they thought allsorts,
sweating profanely.

Granny plays whist
better when pwhist.

Cousin Reggie
who adores the sea
lives in the Midlands
unfortunately.

He surfs down escalators
in department stores
and swims the High Street
on all of his fours.

Sunbathes on the pavement
paddles in the gutter
(I think our Reggie's
a bit of a nutter).

Uncle Philip was hopeless at waterpolo
it just wasn't the game for him
for starters he was colourblind
and besides he couldn't swim.

Banned from English swimming pools
for disobeying basic rules
he emigrated to Eire
where officials were fairer.

From Donegal to Bantry Bay
audiences he astounded
until one fateful Galway day
when his polopony drownded.

If they held Olympic contests
for brick-throwing
Uncle Sean would win them all
at all.

But they don't.
So he carries hods for Wimpeys
and dreams of glories
that might have been.

Uncle Sean lives in Coventry
a stone's throw away
from the Albert Hall
at all.

Frau Eva
wrestled in mud.
At wrestling in mud
she was terribly good.
She wore flimsy
leopardskinleotards
and was much sought
after each rude bout
men queued out
side and vied
to take her home
scrape off the caked mud
and drink liebfraumilch
out of her silk
jackboots.

Angelina
(blueblooded)
owned a yacht
and smoked pacht
a lacht.
So when things
gacht hacht
away sailed Angelina
(so regal)
to where the grass was greener
(and legal).

Uncle Jack
was a very cross
countryrunner.
Nothing seemed
to make him happy.

With only one lung
he couldn't run fast
so he took short cuts
and still came last.

And sadder still
for Uncle Jack
some of the short cuts he took
he never gave back.

34

Uncle Trevor and Aunty Renée
won the Northamptonshire
ballroom dancing championship
seven times on the foxtrot.

Practice makes perfect.
Every night after saying their prayers
they glide round the bedroom
for hours on end.

(The nightdress Aunty Renée
wears, she made herself
out of 250 yards
of floral winceyette.)

Uncle Trevor however,
made of sterner stuff
to's and fro'ze
in the buff.

Cousin Horatio
won a ten pound bet
by rowing across the Pacific
singlehanded. Six months later
he confessed to having used
both hands, and rather
than face public scorn
sailed from Exmouth
one grey dawn
wrote up his log
tidily
then committed himself to the deep
suicidily.

Cousin Fosbury
took his highjumping seriously.
To ensure a floppier flop
he consulted a contortionist
and had his vertebrae removed
by a backstreet vertebraeortionist.

Now he clears 8 foot with ease
and sleeps with his head
tucked under his knees.

Alf
on his day off from Billy Smart's,
tarts himself up. Puts on
his best monkey boots and braces
and races down to Clacton with his mates.
He hates greasers, hippies, pakkies and blacks
(and they don't care much for him either).

Alf
is famous for his fighting skills
and rightly so.
He knocks out teeth with an entrechat
then pirouettes on his toe.
With a flick of the hip
and a backward flip
he blackens eyes. It's no surprise
he's the toast of the south coast
no butts about it.
He handstands on noses
then poses, so bold,
and his somersaults to the groin
are a joy to behold.

Alf
is an aggrobat.

Aunt Agatha
blooded at five
loves to hunt foxes
and eat them alive.
No horsewoman
she prefers to run
with the hounds.

On all fours
shod in running-
gloves and shoes
no dog can match her
and once on the scent
nose smell-bent
no horse can catch her.

And she snaps
and she barks
and she urges the pack
onward on
to her bushy-tailed snack.

Tongue flapping
huntingpink suit
nostrils aflare
beware any hare
caught napping
en route.

And she snaps
and she barks
and she urges the pack
onward on
to her bushy-tailed snack.

D'ye ken Aunt Agatha
in her coat so gay.
D'ye ken Aunt Agatha
at the close of day
houndsurrounded
tearing into foxflesh.

Uncle 'enery
whose career in the ring
spanned almost two rounds
was a boxer of many parts.
He had: nerves of steel
          a will of iron
          a heart of gold
          a jaw of glass
alas.

Old Mac, seventyodd
and eyes akimbo
was a prizefighter
in his youth.

Some nights in the bar
when he's had a few
he'll spar
with ghosts of pugilists
long since counted out.

Old Mac, still in training
for his final bout.

Uncle Terry was a skydiver.
He liked best
the earth spread out beneath him
like a springcleaned counterpane.
The wind his safety net.

He free fell every day
and liked it so much
he decided to stay.
And they say he's still there
sunbathing in the air.

He sleeps each night
tucked up in moonlight
wakes at dawn
and chases clouds.

Living   off   the   food   birds   bring

Uncle   Terry   on   the   wing

away   from   it   all

dizzy   with   joy.

Uncle Jason, an ace in the Royal Flying Corps
grew up and old into a terrible borps.
He'd take off from tables to play the Great Worps
stretch out his arms and crash to the florps.

His sister, an exSister (now rich) of the Porps,
would rorps forps morps: 'Encorps! Encorps!'

Cousin Christ (né Derek)
got out of bed at 8 to meditate.
Lacking a desert, he wandered
on Blackheath for 40 days
and 40 nights before being
arrested by two pharisees
in a panda car. "Father
forgive them" he said.
And father, a door-to-door
used toupée salesman from Lewisham
did.

Cousin Fiona
from near the top drawer
is a blueblood donor
and Kensington bore.

A moderate showjumper
plain and weakwilled
Cousin Fiona
is never funfilled.

For what she wants
and will never admit
is a man to take her by the bit.

Someone to
jog with
snog with
look in her eyes
canter
banter
romanticize
someone to
lead her
to pastures new
someone to
share her
pony-made-for-two.

And Fiona sleeps in a saddlesoaped room
and dreams of a pinstripe-jodhpured groom
and crop in hand, she gallops into moonlit gymkhanas
to ride gentleshod over her sinning nude sinewed broncoing buck
giddyup   giddyup   giddy   up   up   up.

And Fiona weeps after her lonely ride
always a bridle, never the bride.

ping
ping
ping
ping
ping
ping
ping
ping
ping
ping
ping
ping
ping
ping
ping
ping
ping
ping
ping
ping
ping
ping
ping
pong
set

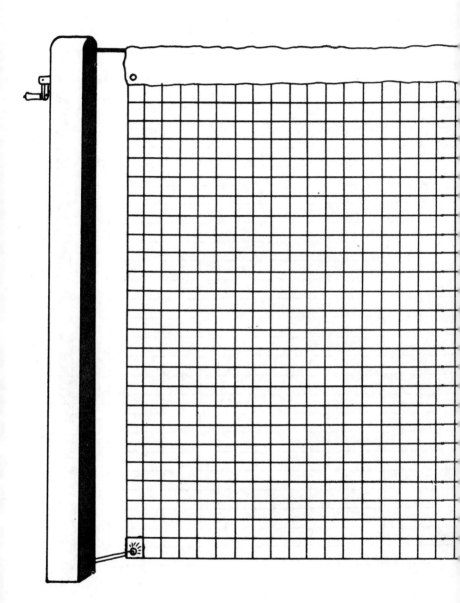

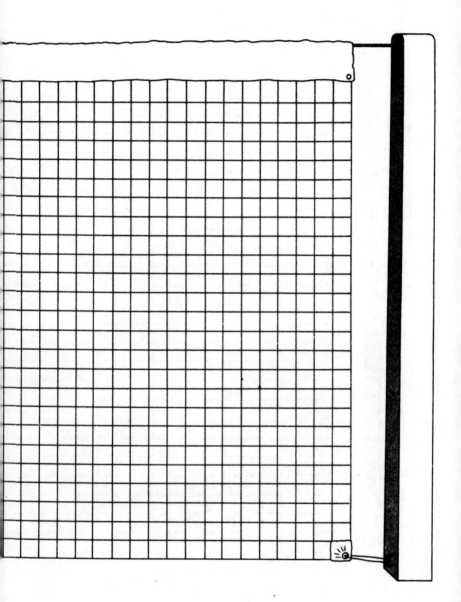

pong
pong
pong
pong
pong
pong
pong
pong
pong
pong
pong
pong
pong
pong
pong
pong
pong
pong
pong
pong
pong
game
match

Big Arth from Penarth
was a forward and a half.
Though built like a peninsula
with muscles like pink slagheaps
and a face like a cheese grater
he was as graceful and fast
as a greased cheetah.

A giraffe in the lineout
a rhino in the pack
he never passed forward
when he should've passed back
and once in possession
s l a a l o m e d his way
through the opposition.

And delicate?
Once for a lark
at Cardiff Arms Park
Big Arth
converted a softboiled egg
from the halfway line.

No doubt about it, he was one of the best players in the second team.

The Hon. Nicholas Frayn
who threw the javelin
would always travelin
a chauffeur-driven plane.
He somewhat lacked a chin
but always threw to win
and was notoriously vain.

He used only monogrammed javelins
sapphire-tipped and silver-plated
and was rated good enough to win his blue.
One day at a meeting in Crewe
he tripped and ran himself through
and though bleeding profusely
from a wound in his side
carried on gamely to finish next to last.
Then died.

Aunt Ermintrude
was determined to
swim across the Channel.
Each week she'd
practise in the bath
encostumèd in flannel.

The tap end
was Cap Gris Nez
the slippy slopes
were Dover. She'd
doggypaddle up and down
vaselined all over.

After 18 months, Aunt Erm was in peak condition.
So, one cold grey morning in March
she boarded the Channel steamer at Dover
went straight to her cabin
climbed into the bath
and urged on by a few well-wishers,
Aunt Ermintrude, completely nude
swam all the way to France.
Vive la tante!

Uncle Leo's sole ambition
was to be a liontamer
so he enrolled for classes at nightschool
and practised at home on his wife.

Aunt Elsa at first had reservations
but having once acquired
a taste for raw meat and the lash
she came on by leaps and bounds.

And after only 6 months
Uncle Leo announced with some pride
that his wife had opened her mouth
and he'd put his head inside.

One afternoon however
while he was changing the sawdust
in the bathroom, Aunt Elsa escaped
mauled 2 boy scouts and a traffic warden
before being captured by the RSPCA.

Now a tamed Uncle Leo, give him his due
visits her daily at Regents Park Zoo.

Uncle Len
a redundant gamekeeper
strangled cuckoos.
He didn't give a f — whose
                    c — oos
he strangled
as long as he silenced
as many as he could.

Last March in Bluebell Wood
while reaching for the season's
first feathered victim
he fell forty feet
broke his neck
and screaming,
unwittingly heralded spring.

Elmer Hoover
on vac from
Vancouver
went fishing
off the Pier Head.

He caught 2 dead rats
dysentery
and a shoal of slimywhite balloonthings
which he brought home in a jamjar.
'Mersey cod' we told him.

So he took the biggest
back to Canada.
Had it stuffed, mounted,
and displayed over the fireplace
in his trophy room.

'But you shudda seen
the one that got away'
he would say.
Nonplussing his buddies.

Cousin Daisy's
favourite sport
was standing
on streetcorners.

She contracted
with ease
a funny disease.
Notwithstanding.

Cousin Nell
married a frogman
in the hope
that one day
he would turn into
a handsome prince.

Instead he turned into
a sewage pipe
near Gravesend
and was never seen again.